Hanukkah

A Level Two Reader

By M. C. Johnston

כל הנשמה
נשיר ונברך

Hanukkah is a holiday for people of the Jewish faith. It is a special time all over the world. It lasts for eight days.

Candles are lit during Hanukkah. They help people remember an important time in Jewish history. The candles stand in a holder called a menorah.

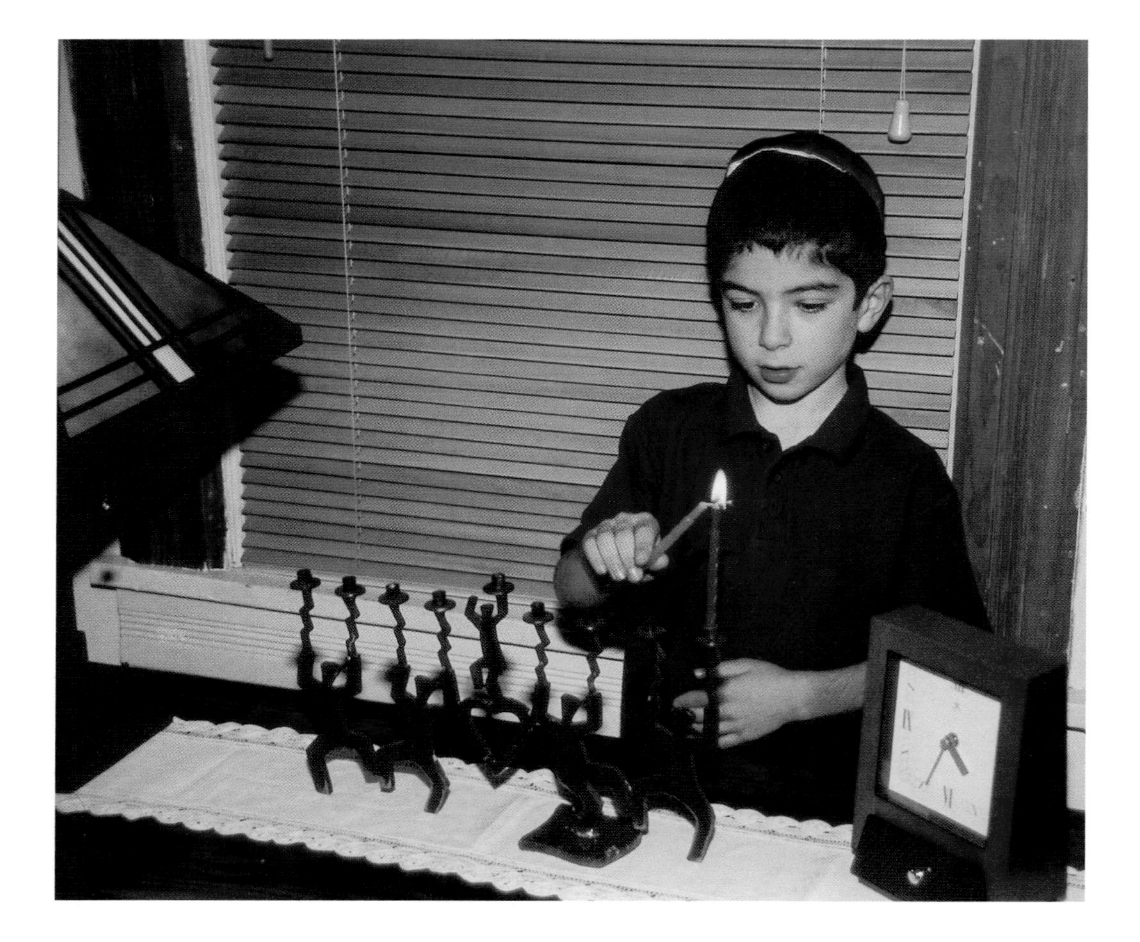

The menorah holds nine candles. The middle candle is used to light the other candles.

On each night of Hanukkah, one candle is lit. By the end of Hanukkah, all of the candles are lit.

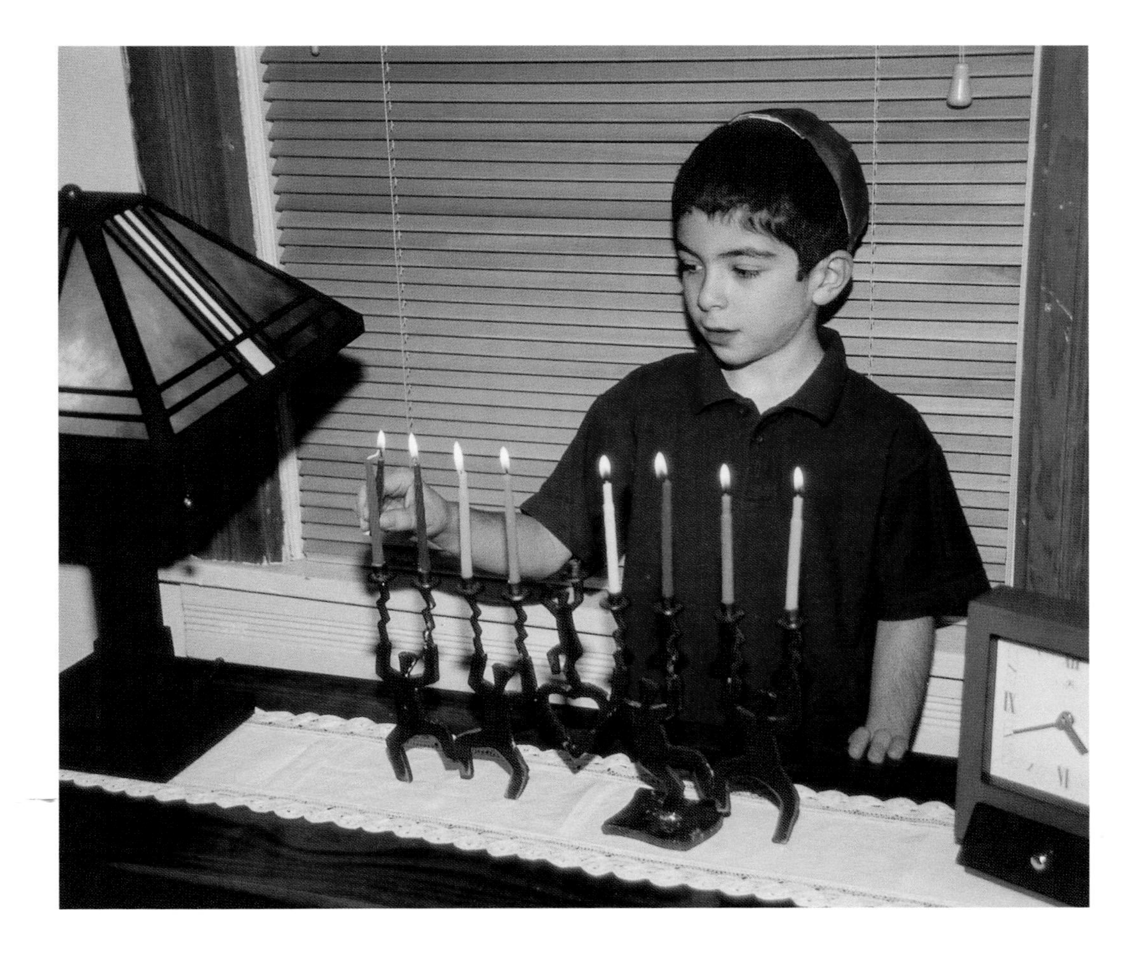

כל הנשמה

People say blessings during Hanukkah. They also give each other gifts.

During Hanukkah, people play a fun game. They use a toy called a dreidel.

GIMEL
ג

People spin the dreidel like a top. The letters on the sides tell who wins the game.

Special pancakes are eaten during Hanukkah. They are called latkes.

Jelly doughnuts are eaten during Hanukkah, too. The latkes and doughnuts are cooked in oil.

Hanukkah is a special time.

Happy Hanukkah!

Index

To Find Out More

Books

Manushkin, Fran. *Hooray for Hanukkah.* New York: Random Library, 2001.

Ross, Kathy. *Crafts for Hanukkah (Holiday Crafts for Kids).* Brookfield, Conn.: Millbrook Press, 1996.

Schotter, Roni. *Hanukkah!* New York: Little Brown & Co., 1993.

Web Sites

Kids Domain
http://www.kidsdomain.com/holiday/chanukah/
An explanation of Hanukkah and lots of fun activities.

Torah Tots
http://www.torahtots.com/holidays/chanuka/chanuk.htm
More activities to help you learn about Hanukkah.

Note to Parents and Educators

Welcome to Wonder Books®! These books provide text at three different levels for beginning readers to practice and strengthen their reading skills. Additionally, the use of nonfiction text provides readers the valuable opportunity to *read to learn*, not just to learn to read.

These leveled readers allow children to choose books at their level of reading confidence and performance. Nonfiction Level One books offer beginning readers simple language, word choice, and sentence structure as well as a word list. Nonfiction Level Two books feature slightly more difficult vocabulary, longer sentences, and longer total text. In the back of each Nonfiction Level Two book are an index and a list of books and Web sites for finding out more information. Nonfiction Level Three books continue to extend word choice and length of text. In the back of each Nonfiction Level Three book are a glossary, an index, and a list of books and Web sites for further research.

State and national standards in reading and language arts emphasize using nonfiction at all levels of reading development. Wonder Books® fill the historical void in nonfiction material for primary grade readers with the additional benefit of a leveled text.

About the Author

M. C. Johnston started her career as a book editor and designer. Since then, she has written many books for young children. She currently lives in Minnesota.

Published by The Child's World®, Inc.
PO Box 326
Chanhassen, MN 55317-0326
800-599-READ
www.childsworld.com

Special thanks to the Rosen family for welcoming us into your home and allowing us to photograph your celebration.

Photo Credits
All photos © Romie Flanagan

Project Coordination: Editorial Directions, Inc.
Photo Research: Alice K. Flanagan

Printed in the United States of America.

Library of Congress Cataloging-in-Publication Data
Johnston, M. C., 1973–
Hanukkah / by M. C. Johnston.
p. cm. — (Wonder books)
Summary: A simple introduction to the meaning and celebration of Hanukkah.
ISBN 1-56766-024-X
1. Hanukkah—Juvenile literature. [1. Hanukkah. 2. Holidays.]
I. Title. II. Wonder books (Chanhassen, Minn.)
BM695.H3 J59 2001
296.4'35—dc21
2001007943